Edmund Burke

A General Reply to the Several Answerers

A letter written to a noble lord, by the Right Honourable Edmund Burke

Edmund Burke

A General Reply to the Several Answerers
A letter written to a noble lord, by the Right Honourable Edmund Burke

ISBN/EAN: 9783337195618

Printed in Europe, USA, Canada, Australia, Japan

Cover: Foto ©Andreas Hilbeck / pixelio.de

More available books at **www.hansebooks.com**

A

GENERAL REPLY

TO THE SEVERAL

ANSWERERS, &c.

[PRICE TWO SHILLINGS.]

A

GENERAL REPLY

TO THE SEVERAL

A N S W E R E R S, &c.

OF A

LETTER Written to a NOBLE LORD,.

BY THE RIGHT HONOURABLE

EDMUND BURKE.

———————

L O N D O N:

PRINTED FOR ALLEN AND WEST, NO. 15, PATERNOS-
TER-ROW.

1796.

A

GENERAL REPLY, &c.

POLITICAL inveſtigation, if at all con-
nected with meaſures immediately before
the Publick, never fails to involve an infinity
of miſrepreſentation : much of it ariſing from
ignorance and perverſion of facts and circumſtances; much from the ſpirit of party, ever
more emulous of propagating its tenets, than
of elucidating their propriety ; and much from
a ſort of perſonal enmity cheriſhed by weak
people againſt thoſe whoſe principles and per-
ſuaſions embrace objects not within the pale of
their eſtimation.

From

From thefe and fimilar fources, Mr. Burke could not but have reafon to expect a deluge of trafh on the fubject of his late Letter ; and he has not been difappointed.

His Reflections on the French Revolution gave birth to innumerable and extraneous publications : innumerable, as the fubject necef-farily engaged the attention of the whole world ; extraneous, as fcarcely any of his commentators omitted to honour his work with annotations as invidious and perfonal, as they were injudicious and foreign to the nature of the inquiry. Such being a part of the ef-fects produced by the Reflections, the Letter to a Noble Lord, affording fome pretext for per-fonal difquifition, could not fail of calling forth the powers of thofe who fancy themfelves poffeffed of political acumen, when their minds are only irritated by political afperity. The confequences have been conformable. The writers feem lefs anxious, and certainly lefs able, to trace Mr. Burke's conduct and prin-ciples, than to expofe their own. With what-ever intention they may have written, they have proved how much ftronger are their paffions

fions and prejudices than their means of knowledge, or their powers of logick. In remark-
ing on Mr. Burke, they have difcovered how
eafy it is for men to libel themfelves.

Among Mr. Burke's opponents it feems a
matter of controverfy, whether he merited the
Penfion, which has given rife to this warfare,
for fervices long fince performed,* or for fervices

---

* " Far be it from me to depreciate the value of Mr.
" Burke's *former* fervices; or to detract from the merit of
" his *former* labours. I never can forget, and the nation never
" can forget, the noble manner in which he ftood up du-
" ring the American war, in defence of thofe rights of man
" which he has fince fo ftrenuoufly queftioned and attacked.
" —You will obferve that Mr. Burke refts all his claim
" to compenfation upon his *former* fervices."

*A Vindication of the Duke of Bedford's Attack upon
Mr. Burke's Penfion. By Thomas George Street.*

Thus becaufe fome of Mr. Burke's *former* fervices cor-
refponded with the political ideas of this Mr. Street, and
becaufe fome of thofe fervices, though conftitutional, were
ignorantly fuppofed to be inimical to the interefts of the
Crown, and *therefore*, no doubt, highly gratifying to the
fame Mr. Street, he is lavifh in his commendations of a
conduct which another opponent virulently condemns.

" You

vices of a later date, or whether he merited it
at all. On thefe points the literary Remarkers
are by no means agreed. They, however,
unite in giving him credit for talents which
he, perhaps, does not poffefs in the eminent
degree they are fo willing to allow. The arguments which they cannot confute they
would fain perfuade their readers have nothing
to recommend them but the ftyle of the com-
pofition: fo that the excellence which they

" You fteadily," fays. M. C. Browne, " fupported the
principle of our *right* to tax America." So that, after all,
Mr. Burke was not defending the " rights of man" in that
bufinefs: he was confiftently defending the conftitutional
rights of Great Britain. But he does *not*, as this Mr. Street
takes upon him to affert, " reft *all* his claim to compenfation upon his *former* fervices." He believes all his late
fervices, as they were equally well meant and conftitutional,
equally entitled to publick approbation. And if Mr.
Burke's principles during the American war were fuch as
Mr. Street *admires*, and thofe which Mr. Burke maintained refpecting the French revolution be fuch as Mr. Street
" *detefts*," the political reputation of Mr. Burke ought to
fuffer no injury, and indeed cannot fuffer any injury, from
the impeachments of men fo prone, from paffion or prejudice, to make broad diftinctions where there is no fhade of
difference.

pretend

pretend to compliment in the firſt inſtance,
is, in the next, brought to counteract its own
efficacy. But with ſuch writers this is nothing
new. Of the praiſe which they beſtow on
their adverſary they always hope to participate
by reflection. It is a pity that they ſo ſeldom
ſucceed.

Whatever may be Mr. Burke's merits theſe
gentlemen ſeem as incapable of combining
them as the Duke of Bedford is of appreciating
them. To ſome act of his life each of them
appears willing to allot ſome portion of approbation. A meaſure long ſince purſued, a
conduct adopted at a given period, on a particular occaſion, is recurred to as an act of
patriotiſm ; not for the intention with which
it was then embraced, or the effect which it
then produced ; but becauſe the like meaſure,
or a ſimilar conduct, might at this moment
contribute to the accompliſhment of projects
as inimical to the political welfare of the country, as at the former period they may have
been found ſalutary. I allude to no ſpecifick
inſtance. Who; except ſuch partial and ſu-
perficial reaſoners, does not know, that to
profecute

profecute any meafure beyond certain limits, is
to defeat the propofed end?

But it is not fo much Mr. Burke's Penfion
that excites the furor of the Bedfords and the
Lauderdales, as his principles. It is confeffed,
that he is not fo much cenfured for accepting,
as the minifters are criminated for beftowing,
rewards on a man whofe conduct and whofe
writings are found to operate againft the views
of thofe who wifh to tolerate, in this country,
French principles and French freedom. And
in order to render him and his penfion the
more obnoxious, he is reprefented as having
renounced principles which he formerly held:
that the leading tenets in his book on the
French Revolution are contradictory to thofe
on which he has acted in his parliamentary
capacity; and he is branded with the odium
of that inconfiftency which always implies
political turpitude, and felf-interefted tergiverfation.

Part of this charge arifes from incapacity
in thofe who make it, and part from their
malignity. For what are the points of inconfiftency, and what do they amount to? It
fhould

should seem that Mr. Burke, in expressing his sentiments respecting the Revolutionists of France, had occasion to reprobate their conduct, and to justify that reprobation by describing those excellencies of the British Constitution, and those principles of civil liberty and of political economy which the Revolutionists had violated, or which their system necessarily tended to violate; and without a regard to which it was utterly impossible they should found on any stability a government of any description, at all calculated for a great empire. In executing this task, Mr. Burke is said not only to have mistaken the principles on which the French Revolution was commenced, but to have misrepresented the principles of the British government; and to have promulgated opinions unfriendly to civil liberty, and subversive of his own doctrines on former occasions. He denies it. He contends, and he has, indeed, already made it appear, that neither in his conduct nor in his doctrines has he at all swerved from those Whig principles, which form the basis of that Constitution which it must ever afford him satis-

faction

faction to recollect he has had the honour to defend, as well againft the too powerful influ-ence of the Crown, as againft the encroachments of the People. Every one will recollect his con-duct on the former occafion. But on the lat-ter, his fervices though, as he conceives, no lefs ufeful, becaufe no lefs conftitutional, ap-pear to have been purpofely erafed from thofe tablets which contain the records of fuch acts only as are fuppofed to diminifh the privileges of the higher orders, and to add to thofe of the democratick body of the ftate. Let it be recollected then, that Mr. Burke " was the firft man who, on the huftings, at a popular election, rejected the authority of inftructions from conftituents ; or who, in any place, has argued fo fully againft it. Perhaps the dif-credit into which that doctrine of compulfive inftructions, under our conftitution, is fince fallen, may be due, in a great degree, to his oppofing himfelf to it in that manner, and on that occafion.—The Reforms in Reprefentation, and the Bills for fhortening the duration of Par-liaments, he uniformly and fteadily oppofed for many years together, in contradiction to

many

many of his beſt friends.—He oppoſed thoſe of the church clergy who had petitioned the Houſe of Commons to be diſcharged from the ſubſcription. At the ſame he promoted the clauſe that gave the diſſenting teachers another ſubſcription in the place of that which was taken away.—People at that time could *diſtinguiſh between a difference in conduct, under a variation of circumſtances, and an inconſiſtency in principle* *."

Indeed one might be led to imagine, from the inexhauſtible jargon of Mr. Burke's opponents, that the Britiſh conſtitution doth not conſiſt of Three Eſtates; but that it is a government wholly ſubſervient to the fluctuating will, and fleeting caprices, of the governed. For as long as the principles of a mixed conſtitution be admitted, Mr. Burke can want no more than that admiſſion to "juſtify to conſiſtency every thing he has ſaid and done during the courſe of his political life." In nothing have his adverſaries more expoſed themſelves than in this reiterated charge of inconſiſtency.

* Appeal from the New to the Old Whigs.

Moft of the writers againft the late Letter feem totally ignorant of the fubject. So confcious is Mr. Burke of poffeffing the virtue of con-fiftency, at leaft, that I may fafely repeat what has been elfewhere obferved, that " if he could venture to value himfelf upon any thing, it is on this very virtue of confiftency that he would value himfelf the moft. Strip him of this, and you leave him naked in-deed !"

Weighed in the petty balance, meafured on the narrow fcale, of a mere partizan, it is not Mr. Burke, nor any man who fhall be an active Senator, that can poffibly efcape the ca-lumny of inconfiftency. It is the common catchword of the party, whofe exclufive inte-refts he apparently oppofes for the preferva-tion of the united interefts of all. Added to this, it muft be confidered, that almoft every new queftion raifes a hoft of fpeculative opi-nions : and that in political, as well as in other refearches, men contend full as violently for theory as for practice. Hence it is clear, that " he who thinks that the Britifh confti-tution ought to confift of the three members,

of

of three very different natures, of which it
does actually confift, and thinks it his duty to
preferve each of thofe members in its proper
place, and with its proper proportion of power, muft, as each fhall happen to be attacked,
vindicate the three feveral parts on the feveral
principles peculiarly belonging to them. He
cannot affert the democratick part on the principles on which monarchy is fupported; nor
can he fupport monarchy on the principles of
democracy; nor can he maintain ariftocracy
on the grounds of the one or of the other, or
of both. All thefe he muft fupport on grounds
that are totally different; though practically
they may be, and happily with us they are,
brought into one harmonious body.

A man could not be confiftent in defending
fuch various, and, at firft view, difcordant
parts of a mixed conftitution, without that
fort of inconfiftency with which Mr. Burke
ftands charged †." This may be, and probably is, incomprehenfible, if not to the un-
derftandings, at leaft to the prejudices of Mr.

† Appeal.

Burke's

Burke's detractors. And yet it is a conduct which, in the ordinary concerns of life, is daily adopted by thofe who cannot difcern its political propriety. Judged then by the conftitution, and not by party prejudice: judged by the united body of the ftate, and not by a diftinct member of it only ; judged as a real fupporter of the King, Lords, and Commons, and of the refpective powers and prerogatives of each, and not as the varying follower of men and names ; in fhort, judged by principle and not by paffion, Mr. Burke is, perhaps, the laft man in. this country that fhould be taxed with inconfiftency. Brought thus to the teft, even the various paffages in his works " upon very multifarious matter," which have been moft abfurdly deduced * as proofs of mercenary tergiverfation will be found to evince conftitutional confiftency and political rectitude. If they are otherwife underftood, the head of the reader muft be ftrangely influenced by the perverfions of his heart :

---

* See a Letter to H. Duncombe, Efq. by William Miles,

Though

Though it requires no great skill so to select and garble the sentences of a writer as to make him apparently guilty of contradictions the most gross, and of positions the most indefensible. And this, indeed, is by no means uncommon among a certain class of wtiters, whose chief aim is to solicit vulgar applause by giving countenance to vulgar slander*. But it is, literally, like the clown, " speaking more than is set down to him," and is a " most pitiful deception in the fool that useth it."

On the general charge of inconsistency much common place declamation has been used; but by no one fact or argument, has it yet been proved. Considering the impressions the conduct of the French must have made on the mind of Mr Burke; and that, writing

---

* This has been done with great dexterity by Mr. Burke's opponents, and even by way of MOTTO to W. Miles's Pamphlet. It is exactly of a piece with that species of quotation which the pious and learned Author of the " Letters on Infidelity" mentions as the deistical mode of proving from Scripture not only the lawfulness but the duty of SUICIDE: " Then Judas went out and hanged himself— Go thou and do likewise!".

under

under thofe impreffions, he might very eafily
and very naturally have been feduced into opinions and expreffions not exactly conformable
to the ideas he had always taught as a lover of
liberty; it is a fact not lefs fingular than honourable to him, that in his " Reflections"
he has never permitted his paffions to run
counter to his principles. And he has repeatedly challenged, † and does yet challenge,
thofe who affert the contrary, to fhew,
" on what part of that publication, or on
what expreffion that might have efcaped
him in that work, is any man authorized
to charge Mr. Burke with a contradiction to
the line of his conduct and to the current
of his doctrines? The pamphlet is in the
hands of his accufers, let them point out the
paffage if they can."

A writer indeed of fome talent*, and whofe
well-drawn character of the late Queen of
France fo exactly accords with Mr. Burke's

† See Appeal.

* See Mr. Burke's Conduct and Pretenfions Confidered,
&c. By a Royalift.

ideas

ideas of that illuftrious Princefs, has taken occafion to affert, that " it was by an unre-
" mitting difplay, in the Houfe of Commons,
" of fuch talents and fuch principles as Mr.
" Burke poffeffes, that this country loft Ame-
" rica. And that *Paine* has clearly deduced
" the origin of the French Revolution, and
" confequently all its enormities, from the
" inflammatory harangues and democratick
" pofitions at that time diffeminated with all
" poffible induftry, and maintained with all
" poffible tenacity, by this grand leader of
" oppofition. And it is not lefs true than
" fingular, that, in the fpace of a few years,
" all thofe powers of Eloquence which were
" exerted to the utmoft in favour of the Re-
" bellion and Revolution of America, fhould
" be turned, with equal vigour, and with
" equal ardour, againft the very principles
" and the very arguments from which the
" French imbibed that rebellious turpitude
" and revolutionary rancour which have fitted
" them to enjoy, with a fort of diabolical en-
" thufiafm, the execration of the furrounding
" univerfe." The writer has fallen into an

error

error not uncommon among thofe who deal in general pofitions ; who imagine that there is a fimilarity between the American conteft and the French Revolution, becaufe the profeffed object of each was the attainment of unpof-feffed liberty, or the refumption of violated rights : and that he whofe opinions were fa-vourable to the caufe of America muft, to be confiftent, efpoufe that of the French. But the cafes are widely different. Indeed that of France admits of no comparifon with any thing, in the fhape of reformation, revolution, or national convulfion, that has preceded it. It ftands alone. It is one of thofe gigantick monftrofities which may long have been hatching in the womb of Time, but which being fuddenly brought forth, aftonifhes and terrifies. It is an entirely new object of con-templation. It mocks the line and compafs of all political calculation. It overwhelms and confounds all the powers of the mind. The light of philofophy, the learning of ages, and the wifdom of the wife, teach us nothing on this topick ; they are loft in vague furmife and imbecile conclufions. Whatever might

have

have been Mr. Burke's conduct refpecting America, no perfon was warranted in calling upon him to fupport the French Revolution. It is one thing to endeavour to compromife between a mother country and her colonies on the principles of eftablifhed government, and it is another to abet the extermination of all religious, all moral, and all focial order from a vaft Empire, feeking liberty ; but feeking it among the dregs of a flagitious philofophy, and in the very kennels of the moft polluted licentioufnefs. After due inquiry, it will be found, that, on the fubject of the American war*, Mr. Burke " never had any opinions which he has fince had occafion to retract, or which he has ever retracted." And if he could at all hope for candour, the language and the opinions he then held would be found not only confiftent with Whig principles, but with the language and opinions he has ever held, and will ever continue to hold. . If thofe who take the trouble of comparing the

_ * See the Appeal, where the matter is treated at large, and the reprefentations of Mr. Burke's adverfaries confuted.

fenti-

fentiments Mr. Burke has uttered at different periods, and on different occafions, cannot reduce them to the ftandard of the Conftitution, and of Whig principles, he has only to lament that their powers of difcrimination are fo infinitely furpaffed by thofe of their prejudices.

On all great conftitutional queftions it appears that no man can be entitled to the praife of confiftency from the politicians that form the body of Mr. Burke's commentators, but fuch as having once fupported a popular meafure;—they will not recollect that all meafures are popular that are conftitutional;—fhall ever afterwards fupport the democratical part of the community in every meafure, and on every occafion, however adverfe to the fpirit of that Conftitution, which, they will not recollect, is " made up of *balanced powers*." And they not lefs violently than abfurdly, eftimate a man's enmity to the freedom of his country, in proportion to the occafional fupports which, in his political capacity, he muft neceffarily give to the ariftocracy and the monarchy ; that is, to each part of the Conftitu-

tion,

tion, as it fhall happen to be attacked. For fuch politicians there can be no apology that is not founded in hypocrify or ignorance. Either they do not comprehend the fyftem they pretend to admire; or they feek its de-ftruction, by mifreprefenting the principles of the Government, and the conduct of the Governors.

But the charge of inconfiftency more im-mediately urged againft Mr. Burke, is with refpect to Economy. His Grace of Bedford feems to think that Mr. Burke, in accepting of his Penfion, has departed from his own ideas and his own fyftem on this fubject. This, being the direct occafion of Mr. Burke's late letter, is in that letter fully refuted. And the only conclufion to be drawn from a can-did difquifition is, that his Grace, however practically adroit in the management of an ample fortune, fo as to acquire a reputation for great prudence and uncommon difcretion, has not fufficiently ftudied the fcience of poli-tical economy to judge of that which he con-demns. He is yet but a young Senator. The inquiry his Grace would inftitute would be

ufelefs,

uſeleſs, ſince it could afford no information, but to thoſe who, like the noble Duke and the Earl of Lauderdale, either could not, or would not, comprehend the nature or the extent of the ſervices for which Mr. Burke's penſion was granted. Their curioſity is now gratified. They have more information than their pro- jected inveſtigation could have produced. I forbear to ſay any thing of the indecency to- wards the Crown which ſuch an inquiry im- plies. Becauſe I am not ſure that ſuch an in- decency was not included in the motive for diſcuſſion.

If then, and ſurely of that there can remain no doubt, Mr. Burke has uniformly, and ſtre- nuouſly, and conſiſtently defended the Conſti- tution, as compoſed of King, Lords, and Commons, in many years ſervices, and under many trying circumſtances, let not the unſoli- cited remuneration of a gracious Sovereign, who has witneſſed and approved of his exer- tions, become matter of reproach to him. He cannot but deem it equally honourable to the country and to himſelf. Indeed, ſome of his adverſaries admit that he has deſerved

well

well of the Publick : that he has merited his
penfion* : but they contend that it fhould have

* Even one of the *Hackney* fchool, amidft his *claffical
fulminations* againft Mr. Burke, fays, ' As to the penfion
' of Mr. Burke, if the prefent Minifters, or any other fet
' of men, had come forward to the Parliament and the
' Publick, in a tone, frank, manly, and explicit : " Mr.
" Burke, for a confiderable portion of his life, has devoted
" in his fenatorial capacity, thofe talents and accomplifh-
" ments,

 " Of which all Europe rings from fide to fide,"

" to the fervice of the State, and has benefited his coun-
" try, in fome important inflances : it is our wifh to re-
" compenfe the merits of fo great a man, and to provide
" for the repofe of his declining years, in a publick re-
" numeration, fanctioned by the fuffrage of his country ;
" and we apply to that country for this purpofe." If, I
' fay, a propofal of fuch a nature had been made, and
' in fome fuch manner ; no man, I venture to affert, would
' have hefitated a fingle fufpicion of diflike. All parties
' and defcriptions * could not have failed to join in their
' applaufe of a meafure, apportioned with difcretion, **not**
' lefs honourable to the donors, than the fubject of it.'

 Wakefield's Reply to Mr. Burke's Letter.

* This author, who writes " by the card," it is prefum-
ed here means " Every party :" for though " *all* parties
and defcriptions could not have failed"—*fome* might.

been

been conferred by Parliament. It is the peculiar and conftitutional province, as it is the gracious pleafure, of the Crown, to reward thofe Servants of the Publick, whofe labours entitle them to fuch diftinguifhed approbation. And it is no lefs the province and conftitutional right of Parliament to canvafs this as well as every other act of Government. Mr. Burke knows this: He has afferted and maintained it. His late Letter implies no queftion of this right. He meant that letter as fuch a juftification of his acceptance of a Penfion as the Duke of Bedford's attack feemed to require.

In one thing, at leaft, will the fapient annotators on Mr. Burke allow him the virtue of confiftency in its utmoft latitude. They uniformly afcribe to him a predilection for *Popery:* and he is favoured with all the grofs epithets which modern liberality fo abundantly lavifhes on blind fuperftition. It is always the fate of cunning, as well as of folly, to overfhoot its mark. Becaufe Mr. Burke has expreffed, and that with a warmth and vehemence becoming the occafion, thofe fentiments which furely every good mind muft feel, for the calamities

nities inflicted on a body of people employed as the miniftry of a national religion, he is
directly accufed of maintaining the principles
of that religion, of fubfcribing to its doctrines, of fupporting its errors, of being himfelf a member of its community. As if it
were impoffible or improper to feel for the
miferies of mankind, and to execrate the au-
thors of boundlefs mifchief, without counte-
nancing the follies, and defending the fpeculative abfurdities, of thofe who fuffer. That
religion is particularly obnoxious to this Government, and in this Country. Hence is
Mr. Burke, in common with many high and
diftinguifhed characters, who love their country, and revere the Eftablifhment, calumniated,
as holding religious tenets fubverfive of that
political creed, on the faith and obfervance of
which is built the fuperftructure of our national felicity. It was referved for thofe profound fcrutinizers of the human heart, the
doctors of the philofophy of new lights, to
difcover in a fcholar of the Eighteenth century,
opinions long fince exploded, and doctrines
which even Ignorance herfelf has long fince
difowned.

difowned. But the tafk is as eafy, as it is
common, to attribute obliquity of mind to
thofe whofe actions are not fufficiently repre-
henfible to anfwer the purpofes of detraction.
Though we cannot make a conduct, we can
fabricate a creed. And it is wonderful with
what facility a " maker of books" can fwell
his libels * when he once affumes this privi-
lege of looking with the eyes of the new phi-

.

* A curious inftance of this occurs in " A Letter to
" Henry Duncombe, Efq. by William Miles," in which
the deep-read author, to prove Mr. Burke unworthy of his
Penfion, employs many pages and fome very exceptionable
and indelicate language, in defcanting on " miracles, re-
" licks, difpenfations, plenary indulgences, pardons, and
" all the difgufting buffooneries which impofture, aided by
" credulity and power, had contrived, manufactured, and
" converted into ftable, lucrative, merchantable commo-
" dities, for the triple purpofe of enriching a profligate vo-
" luptuous priefthood, cozening the deluded nations of the
" earth, and brutalizing the human fpecies over the whole
' furface of the habitable globe !" All this is very-much
to the purpofe. In proportion, however, as it exhibits the
follies and fuperftitions of Popery, it may ferve to convince
his readers, that William Miles, and others of his way of
thinking, muft entertain an idea that they are *very wife*,
and that Mr. Burke is *very ignorant*.

lofophy

lofophy into the mind of the man he wifhes to defame.

It were a work as endlefs to anfwer, as it is difficult to comprehend, the objections of common-place writers. *Damnant quod non intelligunt.* Indeed they generally carry their own confutation. What, one might afk, fhall be faid to fuch as read Mr. Burke's Reflections on the French Revolution as a defence of " difcarded tyranny and fuperftition* ?" Evidently they cannot at all underftand either the intention or the words of the Author. To reply to fuch writers is to multiply books without advancing knowledge. It is in vain to direct the arrows of Reafon againft the united fhields of prejudice and folly.

To be at all attached to any form of Government, or to any religious Eftablifhment, tending to controul that licentioufnefs which deceives with a fhew of liberty, is a crime fufficient to draw down the vengeance of the fans-culotte philofophers. " To fear God; " to look up with awe to Kings; with af-

* Miles's Letter.

E, " fection

" fection to Parliaments; with duty to Ma-
" giftrates; with reverence to Priefts; and with
" refpect to Nobility* ;" includes, it fhould
feem, the whole code of fuperftition : and he
muft needs be wedded to Popery, and an
enemy to the human race, who does not lend a
helping hand to effectuate the demolition of the
fabricks that are raifed on thefe foundations.
And yet, fuch is the inconfiftency of fuch philofophy, they who are loud in their cries againft
this order of things, and as fedulous as they
are infidious in their attempts to abolifh thefe
religious, thefe rational, thefe neceffary diftinctions, without which no Government can fubfift, no fociety can be formed; they, I fay,
who would break thefe bonds that keep the
world in order, who would loofe the filver
cord that binds us in civilization, and are dili-
gent to deftroy the harmony of the univerfe;
they are vehement in contending for the purity
and the excellence of the Britifh Conftitution !—with their lips they praife it, though
their hearts are fet on its deftruction. It is

* Reflections.

an

an artful and a wicked policy, highly worthy of the new fect, alternately to extol and to degrade, the better to accomplifh the project of fubverfion.

Well, indeed, may Mr. Burke be ftigmatifed with fcurrilities by thofe who, adopting the dogmas and the language of a philofophy at war with nature, regard Religion as a mere engine of State. He has ventured to record far other fentiments on this important topick *. " We know," he fays, " and what is better, we feel inwardly, that religion is the bafis of civil fociety, and the fource of all good and of all comfort. In England we are fo convinced of this, that there is no ruft of fuperftition, with which the accumulated abfurdity of the human mind might have crufted it over in the courfe of ages, that ninety-nine in an hundred of the people of England would not prefer to impiety. We fhall never be fuch fools as to call in an enemy to the fub-

* Reflections.

ftance

ftance of any fyftem to remove its corrup-
tions, to fupply its defects, or to perfect its
conftruction. If our religious tenets fhould
ever want a further elucidation, we fhall not
call in Atheifm to explain them. We fhall
not light up our temple from that unhal-
lowed fire. It will be illuminated with
other lights. It will be perfumed with other
incenfe than the infectious ftuff which is im-
ported by the fmugglers of adulterated metaphyficks. If our ecclefiaftical eftablifhment
fhould want a revifion, it is not avarice or
rapacity, publick or private, that we fhall
employ for the audit, or receipt, or appli-
cation of its confecrated revenue. Violently
condemning neither the Greek, nor the
American, nor, fince heats are fubfided, the
Roman fyftem of religion, *we prefer the*
PROTESTANT; not becaufe we think it has
lefs of the Chriftian religion in it, but becaufe, in our judgment, it has more. WE
ARE PROTESTANTS, *not from indifference, but
from zeal.*" In what refpect Mr. Burke's
Proteftantifm differs from that of his opponents, may readily be conceived. Though
he

he protests against the tenets and the spirit
of the Church of Rome, he does not protest
against the injunctions and the commands
of God. He reverences the scriptures. He
doubts not their divine original, though
they enjoin submission to higher powers,
and obedience to Kings.

We know that libertines and free thinkers,
under the various denominations of athiests,
deists, and dissenters, have long attacked,
and continue to attack, in every possible mode,
and with every possible weapon, which the
cunning and chicane of disaffection can de-
vise, not alone our religious establishment, not
Christianity only, but every religious code
that inculcates doctrines inimical to the
private purposes and political heresies of
those who hold the natural equality of man,
and his final extinction in the grave. We
know, that possessing such principles, and
despairing to obtain those situations in the
community which interest and ambition
prompt them to covet, they conceive, and
they cherish, an inveterate malignity, like
that of Lucifer viewing Paradise, against
the

the fyftem that excludes them from the full enjoyment of that focial happinefs and thofe municipal advantages incident to unfeigned loyalty and political honefty. Hence is it that they join with atheiftical, and with men of the moft profligate principles; trufting, under the pretext of reform and improvement, to overthrow our national eftablifhments, civil and ecclefiaftical. And like the elegant, but fceptical Gibbon, who regarded Chriftianity but as an innovation on the ancient Pagan worfhip, and therefore endeavoured to fap its foundations, and undermine its authority; fo thefe internal enemies to our happy Conftitution meditate its deftruction, as an infringement on the natural rights of man. They would have us abolifh all the inftitutions produced by the legiflative wifdom of ages; becaufe under thofe inftitutions they cannot gratify the depraved paffions and felfifh appetites which it is the chief object of all civilization to check and controul. To thofe laudable reftraints which make man happy in fpite of his own nature; to thofe compacts which, as the grand efforts of reafon,

fon, fo eminently diftinguifh us from the creatures that furround us; to thofe affociating principles and political unions which bind, and unite, and ftrengthen all perfonal and all focial felicity; they would prefer the natural rights of man: thofe enviable rights which our painted anceftors enjoyed in common with the beafts of the field and the fowls of the air.

Thofe who will not join in this retrograde march to freedom; who think it " good for us to be here;" who in oppofition to the retreats of this indefinable liberty, prefer churches and palaces and the chearful haunts of men, though marked with the lines of fubordination and the divifions and fubdivifions of civilized inequality; thofe are the devotees of ufurped power, the " defenders of tyranny and fuperftition." Be it fo. Applied by fuch men, and on fuch occafions, the language of reproach reflects honor on the cenfured in proportion to its violence.

But how fhall precept fucceed when example fails? The French have fhewn us the
way

way to their temple of liberty. They have illumined the path with conflagrations more glaring than a thoufand comets. The moft diftant realms have been fcorched by the blaze. They have facrificed hecatombs to their goddefs. Her domains are drench-ed in the coftly blood of Princes; her rivers overflow with the gore of millions of fub-jects. Her terrifick voice is heard in every wind; fhe tyrannizes in every bofom. She aims at the fovereignty of the world: her janizaries, armed with power irrefiftible, bow every neck and bend every knee to this crimfon Coloffus, fupported by the rights of man. And is this the Idol we are called upon to worfhip?—the liberty fo proudly contrafted with Britifh free-dom?

" Is this the region, this the foil, the clime,
" ——————————————this the feat,
" That we muft change for heav'n; this mournful gloom
" For that celeftial light ‡ ?"

‡ Milton.

That

That the principles of the French Revolution fhould have engendered this monfter is not ftrange. And yet we are told, with never-ceafing falfehood, and in direct contradiction to what we fee and what we feel, that " thefe principles are good *." And we are ftunned with the applaufes vociferated in honour of the metaphyfical politicians and fans-culotte philofophers, who have had the ingenuity not only to frame fuch a variety and fuch difcordant codes of legiflation, but to referve to themfelves the moft abfolute authority for carrying them into execution. The effects we have feen, and have been compelled to feel. Neither have the tributes of approbation which they folicited been withheld. Our Revolutionary Societies, our demagogues of Chalk-farm, and of Copenhagen-houfe, and of Palaceyard, have been profufe in their teftimonies of admiration. They have, with the true

* Sober Reflections on Burke's Letter, by John Thelwall.

F   fans-

fans-culotte authority, taken the proxies of the kingdom at large. They have anticipated the fraternal embrace. They " have been long prepared to hail the tri- " umphant entry of a Republican Reprefen- " tative; and to exclaim, with equal fince- " rity and rapture,

" Dicite, Io Pæan! et Io, bis dicite, Pæan!"*

If any thing could augment this fincerity and this rapture, it would be that the Republican Reprefentative fhould be received by a Republican funâionary.

If one might be permitted to judge of caufes by their effeâs, and that it were not a mode of ratiocination incompatible with the new philofophy, the miferies, the calamities, the horrors, the aggregated fum of evil, which France has experienced, and under which fhe now labours, and fhall long fuffer, muft be traced to the operation of

* Wakefield's Reply.

thefe

thefe boafted principles *. What Mr. Burke
fo many years ago predicted has come to
pafs. Not a fingle inference drawn by him
from thofe principles has failed. In him it
was not forefight, it was not prefcience; he
pretends to no prophetical powers. The
principles and the conduct of the French
philofophers and legiflators formed a pro-
blem truly fyllogiftick; they furnifhed the
major and the minor. It required no great
powers of mind to difcover the refult
of rebellion and tyranny and turpitude.
It is not for a banditti to legiflate. It is not
for the governed to govern. It is not for a

* Long before the fans-culotte rulers came into power,
and when the French imagined they were proceeding wife-
ly and fyftematically, Mr Burke had occafion to remark :
" Whether the fyftem, if it deferves fuch a name, now
built on the ruins of the ancient monarchy, will be able to
give a better account of the population and wealth of the
country, is a matter very doubtful. Inftead of improving
by the change, I apprehend that a long feries of years muft
be told before it can recover in any degree the effects of this
philofophical revolution, and before the nation can be re-
placed on its former footing."
Reflections.

F 2   rabble

rabble to comprehend the duties, much lefs
to perform the functions, of a Statefman.
Indeed we have heard much of French
Generals and French Orators: of defperate
men, who, at head of huge armies, equally
defperate, have performed fuch exploits,
and committed fuch ravages as unbridled ferocity can always accomplifh, and unprincipled ambition will always attempt. And
doubtlefs the multitude will hear with rapture, and applaud with enthufiafm, thofe
Orators who fhall defend fuch principles,
and animate them to fuch conduct. But
whence do they imbibe the principles, and
how come they to adopt the conduct? It is
acknowledged that they have produced
confequences that difgrace not France only,
or Europe, but the whole world and all the
human race. Afhamed of this conduct,
though glorying in the principles from which
it fprings, every fallacy of fophiftry has
been exerted to trace it to the former government, and as naturally flowing from the
" old

" old defpotifm*." The old defpotifm was
fufficiently deformed, without covering it with
the hideous garb of Republican philofophy. The
tyrannies of the old defpotifm were very diftinct
from thofe of the new. The diftinction is
feen in their laws; it is felt in their effects.
.The old defpotifm did not authorize, nor
could it have brought about the defolations,
the wickednefs, the unparalleled enormities
which have fo naturally, fo inevitably, and fo
univerfally difgraced the new fyftem.

'To fpeak of a cannibal philofopher is, it
fhould feem, to fpeak of an union that does not
exift. It is, however, a Centaur of no fabu-
lous complexion. Mr. Burke can feel no pro-
penfity to dignify the French rulers with the
title of philofophers. It is an affumption of
their own. They have preferred it to that of
honeft men. But take what appellation beft
pleafes them, what epithet their vanity

---

* " The imbecility of the philofophick, and the ferocity
" of the energetick party, had their remote caufes alike in
" the vices and cruelties of the old defpotifm."

Thelwall's Sober Reflections.

prompts

prompts them to adopt, to do them juſtice we are conſtrained to denominate them " cannibals," and cannibals of the fierceſt kind. They are profeſſors of the rights of man ; they are, ſince they will have it ſo, philoſophers ; but they are neither good men, nor ſound politicians. They have taught us to regard as ſimple truths what we have heretofore contemplated as the frightful fictions, and tremendous hieroglyphicks, of antiquity and romance. They have not only called into exiſtence, but they have employed as their chief agents, the

" Gorgons, Monſters, and Chimeras dire,"

for which Imagination herſelf could ſcarcely find a local habitation or a name.   Under the old deſpotiſm there were MEN* ; and the principle

* Revolutions in States uſually produce *great men.*   It has been juſtly obſerved that this of France has not.   Madame Roland obſerves, that " France was in a manner " deſtitute of MEN.   Their ſcarcity has been truly ſurpriſing in this revolution, in which ſcarcely any thing " but pigmies have appeared.   I do not mean, however, " that there was any want of wit, of knowledge, of learn-
" ing,

principle of honour ftimulated them to do
deeds worthy of men, and of Frenchmen.
The old defpotifm was not degraded by a national barbarity, by a ferocity more than bru-
tal, by flagitioufnefs upon principle, alike infamous to the rulers and to the ruled. The
national character was that of honour and humanity. The government, indeed, was not
only bad in itfelf, but it was corrupt. Means
were taken, and chearfully adopted, to ame-
liorate the Government, and to ftop the current
of corruption. The national affembly did what

" ing, of accomplifhments, or of philofophy. Thefe in-
" gredients, on the corfrary, were never fo common.
" But as to that firmnefs of mind, which John James
" Rouffeau has fo well defined by calling it ' the firft attri-
" bute of a Hero,' fupported by that foundnefs of judg-
" ment, which knows how to fet a value upon things, and
" by thofe extenfive views which penetrate into futurity,
" altogether conftituting the character of a great man, they
" were fought for every where, and were fcarcely any
" where to be found."—To this paffage juftice is done by
one of Mr. Burke's antagonifts, who alfo quotes it, with an
exception in favour of fome of the Mountain party, and
of *Danton* in particular. What Madame Roland has,
however, fo judicioufly obferved, every one muft feel to be
true, without any exception.

became

became wife men and ftatefmen. But the completion of their fyftem, at once falutary and politick, was prevented by their too early diffolution, and the confequent introduction of men far lefs able, and being of inferior orders and capacities, more inclined to thofe republican meafures which proved the overthrow of the monarchy, and accelerated that dreadful innun- dation of horrible and indefcribable mifchiefs immediately refulting from principles which, we are told, with frontlefs audacity, had their origin in the old defpotifm. Under that def- potifm, indeed, there was a Baftille, the abode and bulwark of tyranny ; the foul reproach of the country. There was, indeed, a Baftille ; but there was only one. Every petty prifon was not a prifon of State. The Baftille was not crouded with the greateft men, and the beft citizens. Many, too many, unhappy victims, fome worthy and fome worthlefs, in thofe cells, groaned with unavailing forrow, and died the facrifice of relentlefs cruelty. But the detefted walls of the Baftille never inclofed thoufands of the human race ; one hour hur- ried into its execrable confines, and dragged

the

the next to the fcaffold. All Europe rejoiced in the downfall of the Baftille, as in the deftruction of fomething difgraceful to man. We rejoiced in the defolation of thofe gloomy towers that had, for fo many centuries, intombed even the fpirit of Liberty : but we never dreamt that it fhould prove the Hydra of defpotifm, from which fhould fpring innumerable tyrannies, generating innumerable monfters ; rendering the realms of France " regions of terror," and its government the fcourge of its inhabitants.

The cannibal philofophers, thefe legiflators in blood, all whofe policy confifts in force, and whofe wifdom is carried into effect by the guillotine ; thefe doughty doctors and their daring adherents, would willingly perfuade us, that the Revolutionary principles which they fo much applaud, and fo inceffantly recommend, are thofe " humane, incontro-
" vertible, glorious principles that breathed
" through the fpeeches of the National Affem-
" bly, and enlarged at once the boundaries of
" fcience and philanthropy :" whereas the principles adopted, and the conduct purfued

G

by

by the National Convention, and all the fubfequent rulers, were, and are, as oppofite to
thofe of the firft National Affembly, and they
were exceptionable enough, * as the conditions
and faculties of the refpective bodies of which
they were compofed. And it is not unworthy of
remark, that the conduct of the Rulers has
become more and more incompatible with real
policy, or rather fubverfive of all civil and
moral policy, in proportion as the ruling power
has defcended amongft, or been ufurped by,
the inferior orders of the community. It is
not becaufe there are not in thofe claffes of
fociety men eminent for virtue and talent.
" Let us fpeak like politicians, there is a no-
" bility without heraldry, a natural dignity
" whereby one man is ranked with another,
" another filed before him, according to the
" quality of his defert, and the pre-eminence
" of his good parts." But it is becaufe
the influence of thofe individuals is weak
when oppofed to the will of the multitude,
whofe views they may be feduced to fanction

* See Reflections.

by

by ambition, or, indeed, by the hope of ultimately accomplifhing their own virtuous defigns. It has never yet been known when
Power in the hands of the multitude, or of a
Plebeian faction, has not been moft grofsly a-
bufed: not abufed only, but rendered fubfervient
to the worft of crimes. Individual worth is loft
in that general mafs of corruption; *" that
great enemy of reafon, virtue, and religion, the
Multitude, that numerous piece of monftrofity,
which taken afunder feem men, and the reafonable creatures of God; but confufed together make
but one great beaft, and a monftrofity more pro-
digious than Hydra*."* That the principles
and conduct refulting from fuch a tyranny
fhould be at all confonant with, or derived
from, the defpotifm of an abfolute monarchy,
diftinguifhed for the arts and the polifh of civilized life, is a folecifm which republican declamation will find it difficult to remove.

The teachers of the Rights of Man fhould
recollect the difference between a civilized
ftate and a ftate of nature. They fay that

* Sir Thomas Browne.

G 2   all

all men are born equal. This is their text.
Their comments are voluminous. Their glof-.
faries are without end : but they all tend to
enforce one conclufion, on which they erect
their whole political fyftem ; notwithftanding
it is a conclufion which they cannot but feel
to be politically and morally, naturally and
neceffarily falfe. They infer, that becaufe all
men are born equal, which however, is grant-
ing what they cannot prove, they muft remain
fo. This is the firft chapter of their Charter.
But in no part of the globe can they find this
Charter, either naturally or politically, un-
broken. Even in the woods and wilds of
favage life, in all animated nature, and through
all created fpace, pre-eminence and fubordination prevail. Society does not give
them birth. They are the offspring of Nature,
fulfilling the dictates of Providence. In a
ftate of civilization, that is in a ftate where
Reafon acquires authority, and teaches men
what is beft to be done to improve their being, and enlarge their happinefs, we find them
diverging more and more widely from what
thefe preachers would have us underftand by

natural

natural equality : and every man will become more eminent than his fellow citizens, who shall poffefs in any extraordinary degree, the parts and accomplifhments, the qualifications and requifites, which promote civilization and give to fociety all its advantages and all its charms. Government then begins to affume its legitimate form, and to accord with Nature ; to mark its boundaries, its diftinctions, and difcriminations : to eftablifh the rights of community, meri-torious claims, and individual honours. This is the operation of Sovereign Reafon againft whofe authority they would oppofe the fur-reptitious rights of man *. And this operation produces

---

* " I have ever abhorred, fince the firft dawn of my " underftanding, to this its obfcure twilight, all the opera- " tions of opinion, fancy, inclination, and will, in the affairs " of Government, where only a *fovereign Reafon,* paramount " to all forms of legiflation and adminiftration fhould dictate. " Government is made for the very purpofe of oppofing " that reafon to will, and to caprice, in the reformers, or " in the reformed, in the governors, or in the governed ; " in kings, in fenates, or in people."

Mr. Burke's Letter.

So.

produces in human fociety thofe indifpenfible inequalities which pervade the works of
Nature, and which at once fo admirably diver-
fify and harmonize the whole. It is therefore obferved by Mr. Burke, that though
" *numbers* in a ftate are always of confideration, they are not the whole confideration."
What can be done by numbers, without order
and

So little have the French principles to do with Reafon,
that one of their admirers, after quoting the above paffage,
not without a hint of its *myfticifm* and *nonfenfe*, exclaims,
" In the name of common fenfe how many gods has Mr.
" Burke in his mythology? who is this *Sovereign Reafon?*
" In which of the feven heavens does fhe refide? For he
" has told us [where?] that in this world fhe is no where to
" be found."

Thelwall's Sober Reflections.

It has generally been underftood, that Reafon has acquired her title to fovereignty, and all the honours which fhe in-
herits, from the circumftance of her forming that part of
man which diftinguifhes him from the brute creation, by
which he "approximates nearer to the Gods," and is indeed
the perfection of his nature. Mr. Thelwall by *Sovereign
Reafon* would have us to underftand the " collective reafon
of the *Sovereign People.*" Now the collective reafon of the
Sovereign People, that is, of the People he means, is little
more than a natural inftinct to do mifchief: fo common is
it, in the abfence of this Sovereign Reafon, to miftake evil
for good, and good for evil.

and fubordination ? The French have let us fee what is to be done when there is but little. And do not all ftates, and all bodies of people neceffarily fubfide into order and fubordination, naturally and inevitably producing an ariftocracy, a democracy, and not unfrequently a monarchy ? In all thefe the weight and talents lie in the ariftocracy; becaufe it is by the acquifition of power, acquired by virtues and talents, that the ariftocracy is formed. Whence fuch a power is derived, and how utterly incapable the collective mafs of the People are of acquiring it, will be feen if we at all confider of what it confifts.

" A true natural ariftocracy is not a feparate intereft in the ftate, or feparable from it. It is an effential integrant part of any large people rightly conftituted. It is formed out of a clafs of legitimate prefumptions, which, taken as generalities, muft be admitted for actual truths. To be bred in a place of eftimation; To fee nothing low and fordid from one's infancy ; To be taught to refpect one's felf ; To be habituated to the cenforial infpection of the publick eye; To look early to pub-

lick

lick opinion ; To ftand upon fuch elevated ground as to be enabled to take a large view of the wide-fpread and infinitely diverfified combinations of men and affairs in a large fociety ; To have leifure to read, to reflect, to converfe ; To be enabled to draw the court and attention of the wife and learned wherever they are to be found ; To be habituated in armies to command and to obey ; To be taught to defpife danger in the purfuit of honour and duty ; To be formed to the greateft degree of vigilance, forefight and circumfpection, in a ftate of things in which no fault is committed with impunity, and the flighteft miftakes draw on the moft ruinous confequences ; To be led to a guarded and regulated conduct, from a fenfe that you are confidered as an inftructor of your fellow citizens in their higheft concerns, and that you act as a reconciler between God and man ; To be employed as an adminiftrator of law and juftice, and to be thereby amongft the firft benefactors to mankind ; To be a profeffor of high fcience, or of liberal and ingenuous art ; To be amongft rich traders, who from their fuccefs are pre-

fumed

fumed to have fharp and vigorous underftand-
ings, and to poffefs the virtues of diligence,
order, conftancy, and regularity, and to have
cultivated an habitual regard to commutative
juftice : Thefe are the circumftances of men,
that form what I fhould call a *natural* ariftocracy, without which there is no nation *."

Civil fociety "neceffarily generating this †
ariftocracy," is a ftate of nature : " for man

is

---

* Appeal.

† Though it is not for the French rulers and philofophers,
nor for Mr. Thelwall and the difciples of the new lights,
to difcover any utility, on the contrary, nothing but great
nuifance, and a formidable obftruction to the Rights of
Man, in the ariftocracy ; fome of the writers againft Mr.
Burke do allow that it has its virtues, and may be
found ufeful, even in preferving the rights of the People.
One of them obferves, that the Nobility, " in their collec-
" tive capacity, are placed as a barrier between the ufurpa-
" tions of prerogative, and the clamours of democracy.
" Our hiftory abounds in inftances where they have fuccefs-
" fully withftood both.   To the ariftocracy of England we
" are indebted for no fmall portion of our liberties :—For
" the Magna Charta—For the Reformation, by the pro-
" tection which fome of them afforded, in its early ftages,
" to the perfecuted reformers, and by the fpirit with which

H   " they

is by nature reafonable; and he is never per-
fectly in his natural ftate, but when he is
placed where reafon is beft cultivated, and
moft predominates." The opinions and conduct
of our new philofophers would go to deftroy
this " fair proportion of things;" and, under
an idea of the fovereignty of the People, reduce all government to that chaotic anarchy
from which it has been, and always will be,
the province of reafon, and the object of all
good and great men to refcue human nature :
placing focial and individual happinefs on the
firm bafis of duty, truft, engagement and obligation. But the " majority and the fovereignty of the People" are the magick words
that enchant and miflead the multitude; they
are the catch-words of fedition and rebellion :
and it has been ignorantly by fome, and art-
fully by others, maintained, that the majority
of the People have a right to deftroy all go-

" they refifted the papal ufurpations—For the glorious Re-
" volution, which the Ariftocracy planned and effected,"
&c. &c.

Three Letters to the Rt. Hon. Edmund Burke. By
an Old Whig.

vernment,

vernment, to difpenfe with all duty ; to cancel all obligation, to renounce all engagement. They are taught, "by their infamous flatterers," to believe that their power is irrefiftible and uncontroulable ; and that they can abfolve themfelves from the reftraints of reafon, morality and religion, when fuch is their fovereign will. Doctrines which Mr. Burke has always moft ftrenuoufly denied, and has fully expofed, and irrefragably refuted *; and which but to mention, in the way that they ought to be mentioned, muft fhock the very people they are intended to miflead.

But it feems that Mr. Burke has aimed a dagger at the heart of ariftocracy, and fhaken the foundation of all property : that he who has " fupported with very great zeal, and " with fome degree of fuccefs, thofe opinions, " or thofe old prejudices which buoy up the " ponderous mafs of nobility, wealth and

---

* In the Appeal, in which the leading points of the vulgar fophiftry and popular jargon of Paine are examined ; and refpecting which, as they cannot reply, the lecturers, philofophers, and demagogues, have obferved a profound filence.

H 2   " titles,"

" titles," has, in adverting to the origin of thefe diftinctions in the Houfe of Bedford, counteracted his own exertions, and fubverted his own principles. It is the fate, not to fay the intention, of party zeal to draw extraordinary and contradictory conclufions from the moft fimple propofitions ; and the outcry againft Mr. Burke on this occafion has been as clamorous as it is ridiculous. The Duke of Bedford thought proper, becaufe, as his Grace fays, Mr. Burke's " conduct and writings " have, in an eminent degree, contributed to " create and continue the war, and to caufe " all its confequent enormous expences ;" the noble Duke thought proper to declaim againft His Majefty's Minifters for lavifhing a penfion upon an " avowed advocate of economy." For it does not occur to his Grace that he who labours in the publick caufe of publick economy, and who propofes and carries into effect meafures at once prudent and falutary, is, even on the common fcale of vulgar arithmetick, and in the eftimation of economy itfelf, entitled to fome portion of the emolument arifing from fuch regulations,

had

had he no other claim on publick gratitude. One might have imagined that a penfion granted to a fervant of the Crown, and of the Conftitution, and of the People, and who had ftudied and maintained their refpective interefts and privileges, for fo many years, might have efcaped the animadverfions of the noble Duke, and the Earl of Lauderdale ; both of whom appear to confider it exceptionable, principally as it is given to him who has fupported, and would, to the laft, fupport, that Conftitution and thofe principles which it is one object of the prefent war to preferve, and which it is the great object of the French and their abetters to demolifh : becaufe only in that demolition can they look for fuccefs : and becaufe as long as that Conftitution and thofe principles operate and endure, this Country fhall retain her political confequence, her invincible freedom, her unrivalled fplendour. That Mr. Burke's penfion has not exceeded his defervings, he has, I think, made fufficiently clear in his Letter. It is his Grace's misfortune, and not Mr. Burke's fault, that the noble Duke fhould not

be

be willing, or, as Mr. Burke fays, able to eftimate fuch fervices. I cannot, however,
think fo meanly of his Grace's powers of political calculation. Probably his party prejudices are much ftronger than thofe powers.
I muft think he has talents fuperior to the
petty pamphleteers who have fo officioufly
obtruded their mifconceptions on this occafion,

Scribimus indoĉti doĉtique*.

They cannot conceive that Mr. Burke can
have merited his penfion for eight and twenty
years Parliamentary duty, and a great deal of
it fuch as were enough to weigh down both
the body and the mind; much lefs can they
conceive how Mr. Burke could have earned
his penfion before he fet his foot in Parliament. They have no conception (poffibly
his Grace has none) that, he deferves well of
his country who fhall fo prepare himfelf for
the exercifes of a fenator as to be able, on his
coming into Parliament, to underftand his
duty; to be fitted and " difciplined for poli-

* Horace.

tical

tical warfare." It furely requires no fmall
portion of affiduous refearch, and labour, and·
ftudy to become an active fenator. It is eafy
to comprehend the objects and the policies of
a party. But it requires fomething more to·
form a fenator. " He muft poffefs a fund of·
" knowledge that may enable him to act as
" a part of the legiflature. He muft be well
" acquainted with the hiftory, the conftitu-
" tion, and the laws of the country. He
" muft underftand the forms of bufinefs, the
" extent of the Royal prerogative, the pri-
" vilege of Parliament, the detail of Govern-
" ment, the nature and regulation of the
" finances, the different branches of com-
" merce, the politicks that prevail, and the
" connexions that fubfift amongft the differ-
" ent powers of Europe; for on all thefe
" fubjects the deliberations of a Houfe of
" Commons occafionally turn *." It avails
nothing to have had thefe requifites; to have
been indefatigable in the exercife of them; to
have paffed a life of fevere duty and inceffant

* Smollett.

toil;

toil ; if towards its clofe he, who has thus exerted himfelf, fhall, in the moment he is oppofing defperate factions and flagitious principles, accept of reward from a gracious Prince.
The Bedfords and the Lauderdales will call it
" unparalleled profufion," and vociferate with
equal violence and injuftice on the " enor-
mity" of the grant, and deny the pretenfions
of him to whom it is given. Under the impreffions of fuch cenfure, and not to impede
the progrefs of any inquiry, for that, properly
and fairly made, muft have redounded to the
credit and honour of Mr. Burke, there could
furely be no impropriety in inquiring into the
origin of thofe grants from which the Duke
of Bedford derives his ample poffeffions. But
in doing this, did Mr. Burke retort upon the
noble Duke, by attacking his Grace's right to
thofe poffeffions ? His Grace holds them as
the defcendant of a gentleman who had acquired the favour of a powerful monarch.
" His grants," Mr. Burke has obferved*,
" are engrafted on the publick law of Europe,

* Letter.

" covered

" covered with the awful hoar of innumera-
" ble ages. They are guarded by the facred
" rules of prefcription, found in that full
" treafury of jurifprudence from which the
" jejunenefs and penury of our municipal law
" has, by degrees, been enriched and ftrength-
" ened. The Duke of Bedford will ftand
" as long as prefcriptive law endures." We
are not difputing his Grace's title : it is facred ; it is invulnerable to all things but the
attacks of that revolutionary injuftice, and
thofe furreptitious principles of freedom, a-
gainft the progrefs of which it has been found
expedient, and right, and neceffary to fend
forth our fleets and armies; and againft which,
I hope and truft, the Britifh Conftitution will
wage eternal war. For that enmity can never
ceafe, while the Conftitution lives ; and while
the Conftitution lives his Grace's title is fe-
cure. French metaphyficks cannot undermine it. Englifh fedition cannot fhake it.
The noble Duke calls in queftion Mr. Burke's
pretenfions to his new penfion. Mr. Burke
does not call in queftion his Grace's right to
his old penfions. He does not call in queftion

the pretensions of the Earl to whom they were first granted: He only shews what they were; and contrasts them with his own. He questions not the authenticity of the original claims; but he inquires into the merits of the claimant. His Grace, it is presumed, does not so much attack the prerogative from which Mr. Burke derives his pension, as impeach the *quantum meruit* of the Pensioner. Mr. Burke does not "vex the receptacle of the dead, for evidence against the living*." The characters and pretensions of his ancestors cannot affect his Grace, or disturb his title to their possessions. They must put a construction, equally strange and unwarrantable, on Mr. Burke's remarks who call this elucidation of personal merits an "unprincipled attack upon the peaceful security of all property †." Yet from this forced and absurd construction, this *Ignorantia Elenchi*, the prejudiced commentators have drawn matter of much declamation against Mr. Burke, and en-

* Street's Vindication.

† Thelwall's Sober Reflections.

riched their pages with invective; diſplaying the ingenuity of their cenſorial capacities, by reviling him for principles which he never held, and combating poſitions which he never advanced.

The ſame miſconception, I believe rather aſſumed than real, and the ſame ingenuity is employed to convert Mr. Burke's raillery on the official hiſtorians of the Heralds college, into a diſſertation on the origin of property, and a " diſquiſition on hereditary honours * : they adduce and miſapply, a point of pleaſantry, or an effuſion of irony, as an argument to ſhew Mr. Burke's diſaffection to the ariſtocracy, without which he ſays, " there can be no nation;" and cite it as a " democratick contribution to the labours of Prieſtley and of Paine."†

It has been obſerved, with that degree of ſapience and of malignant inuendo which characteriſes the productions I am now noticing, that the grants to Mr. Ruſſell added

* Mr. Burke's Conduct and Pretenſions Conſidered, &c. *By a Royaliſt.* † Ibid.

not

not to the burthens of the nation. I may afk., did his labours, in any refpect, contribute to the welfare of the nation? Did not " thofe prodigies of profufe donation trample on the mediocrity or humble and laborious individuals," without throwing back on the community any publick benefits that could juftify the receiver, or apologife for the Sovereign? But in afking this, is it meant to " preclude the Duke of Bedford from attacking a profufe or unmerited grant of the Crown?" Is Mr. Burke unwilling to concede to his Grace the right which Mr. Burke is himfelf exercifing? Certainly not. By tracing the fource of his Grace's wealth, is it meant to juftify any fimilar profution? Far from it. The inquiry is as to the *quantum meruit*. That of the noble Duke is not difputed. It is fuch, no doubt, as his habits, his education, and his years, may naturally be fuppofed to produce. But it is not from HIS *quantum meruit* that his Grace derives his poffeffions. They are derived from that of another. And fince the noble Duke contefts the propriety of penfioning Mr. Burke, who has no other claim than

that

that of merit, where is the irrelevancy of con-
trasting such merit with that which formed the
basis of his Grace's fortunes? Mr. Burke has
been censured for not noticing the interme-
diate branches of the House of Ruffell: it is
even infinuated that he is no friend to the Pro-
teftant caufe and the caufe of Freedom (in defence of which he has fpent a long life), in-
afmuch as he has not paid a paffing tri-
bute to the excellence of Lord William Ruffell. But I may afk, did the wealth of the
House of Bedford flow from the blood fhed
by that nobleman on the fcaffold? Is it in
Lord William's merit, or his virtue, or his
patriotifm, that the noble Duke finds the origin of his property? No: but thofe qualities
in one of his Grace's predeceffors gives to his
title an additional ftrength, and a collateral fecurity, no lefs honorable than binding, in the
gratitude of his country. Let us hope that
the noble Duke will give it additional luftre,
by " employing all the energy of his youth,
and all the refources of his wealth, to crufh
rebellious principles which have no foundation

tion in morals, and rebellious movements, that have no provocation in tyranny."

That Mr. Burke's inveſtigations on this ſubject ſhould prove prejudicial to ariſtocracy, or ſhake the foundations of property, is a concluſion not eaſily deducible from the pre- miſes. I muſt repeat, that he is aſcertaining merits, and not ſubverting titles. He is ſaid " to change the reſpect of the multitude for " property into diſguſt ; to let looſe their en- " raged paſſions on that wealth which is the " object of their perpetual envy : and to lend " even to rapine itſelf ſome of the features " and lineaments of juſtice *." There is no- thing capable of changing into diſguſt the ge- neral reſpect for property or power, but the abuſe of it. From the demerits of the firſt Earl of Ruſſell they will feel no claim to at- tack the poſſeſſions of the Duke of Bedford. Nothing can abate their reſpect and reverence for his Grace's property, and the laws that ſecure it, but the infuſion of principles de- ſtructive of all rights, and ſubverſive of all

* Monthly Review for March, 1796.

laws.

laws. Nothing can fhake ariftocracy but the conduct of its own members. If they, like the deteftable Orleans, fhall countenance Plebeian factions, and betray their own intereft; if they fhall renounce their own dignity, and queftion their own privileges; if they fhall affemble the populace, and harangue mobs on momentous points, fit only for the difcuffion of deliberate Councils and grave Senates; if they fhall appeal to judgments which they ought to inform, and to paffions which they ought to controul; it is then indeed, that they " lend even to rapine itfelf fome of the features and lineaments of juftice." Then trembles the " Corinthian capital of polifhed fociety." Then is undermined the deep bafe of hereditary property. If fuch nobles have no defigns againft the peace or the conftitution of their country; and I am willing to allow them good motives, for I pretend not to fearch into the hearts of men; yet are they by this conduct abetting thofe who have. They are abetting the internal enemy. They are ftrengthening the hands of the domeftick foe. This mode of poifoning the minds of the People,

and

and of weakening the energies of Government, is more to be dreaded, and more worthy of reprehenfion, becaufe more dangerous, than tranfmitting to the French convention, revolutionary prefents and feditious refolutions.

Abhorring fuch principles, and cenfuring fuch proceedings, with an indignation not eafily expreffed, and which he could never wifh to exprefs but in terms appropriate to his feelings, Mr. Burke has been accufed of recording the effufions of rafhnefs and anger, rather than the refults of reafon and difpaffionate inveftigation. I cannot envy the critical fagacity, the "cold heads and lukewarm hearts," of thofe who read with a fpirit fo different from that of a writer, as neither to tafte, nor to comprehend; thofe figurative expreffions which ftrength of feeling always produces, and which ferve to illuftrate opinion, and to confirm truth: a mode of expreffion which it is the eafieft tafk of malignity to pervert, and of dulnefs to ridicule. The Reflections on the French Revolution afforded fome fcope for the difplay of thefe minor wits and turbulent politicians, whofe minds are darkened by the

boafted

boasted effulgence of their new lights, and
their hearts hardened by philosophical ferocity.
These are the true sans-culotte criticks. They
not only rejoice in the degradation, the de-
posing, and the murdering of the King and
Queen of France; but their feelings are so
far rarified and subtilized by their metaphy-
sicks which lift them above humanity, as to
hold in high derision all such as contemplate
those dreadful scenes with any sensation of
horror. And he could never hope, nor could
he ever wish, to escape their contemptuous
raillery, who, in lamenting the fate of those
illustrious sufferers, could not but regret the
extinction of that heroick virtue which dis-
tinguished even the days of chivalry; when
ferocity itself was not barbarized and reduced
into system by sentiment; nor the sacred
rights of nature usurped by the factitious rights
of man. The invincible detestation which
Mr. Burke has, in his late Letter, expressed
for the monsters who have perpetrated these
crimes, and who have deluged Europe with
blood; that invincible detestation has, in no
less degree, excited the fury of these philoso-

phical " lovers of mankind," thefe " univerfal patriots," whofe open cry is for Reformation and peace, and whofe private pro-
jeɛts are for innovation and plunder. Happy
muft Mr. Burke be to have merited their enmity, which he ought to confider as additional
proofs that he has " produced fome part of
the effeɛt propofed by his endeavours."

To thefe feelings of the heart, this fervour
of principle, the opponents of Mr. Burke
are unwilling, on any occafion, to affign any
good motive. They can find no apology
for enthufiafm, but in favour of fedition :
no virtue in principle, but as it promotes dif-
content. Even his exertions, his nightly
ftudy and his daily toil, for fo many years re-
fpeɛting the intricate, involved, and compre-
henfive affairs of India, are regarded by
them as petty labours, to accomplifh bafe
purpofes. Such is the extent of *their* in-
quiries; fuch the inference of *their* liberality; fuch the complexion of *their* minds.
Nor could he advert to thefe exertions,
nor to any of his fervices, without being
cenfured

cenfured as an * Egotift, by men who feem
as utterly unacquainted with the fubject, as
they are with decency; and who, in repre-
fenting Mr. Burke as bereft of reafon, and
as the difciple of envy and malignity, and
of all the fouler paffions, do this in terms
to convince the world how admirably they
can pourtray themfelves : for it is not lefs
remarkable than true, that, with very few
exceptions, thefe fagacious, heart-reading
obfervers, have not attributed to Mr. Burke
a fingle mode of abufe with which they have
not loaded their own pages; and in their
endeavours to foar a little beyond the " vi-
fible diurnal fphere" of their vapid declamation,

---

* The venerable Plutarch has enumerated a variety of
cafes wherein a modeft man may even praife himfelf, and
when it is his duty to do fo.—Mr. Burke has, on a fair
and proper occafion, ftated fome of thofe fervices that have
been thought worthy of the remuneration which he has received. Is it becaufe they cannot contradict the facts that
the pamphlet-writers are fo eager to depreciate the merits;
and afcribe to Mr. Burke a difgufting degree of felf-praife ?
But we hear nothing of this when the gentlemen fpeak of
Mr. Burke's *former* fervices, *i. e.* of fervices, which, though
done on the great fcale of national good, happened to cor-
refpond with the minutiæ of *their* politicks.

mation, one may well fay of them, as the incomparable Dunning, in his Letters of Junius, faid of Sir William Draper, that they poffefs the " melancholy madnefs of poetry, without its infpiration." And in point of Egotifm, without any pretenfions to publick notice, how infinitely do they furpafs Mr. Burke !—how continually are we reminded of the purity of their principles, and the virtues of their independence !—of worthlefs penfioners, and of unconftitutional penfions! They feem to have generated in their minds an antipathy to the word penfions. One of them, indeed, after enumerating the advantages refulting from " landed penfions," takes notice to remark, * that Penfions fuch as Mr. Burke's " cannot well be " applied to purpofes of national improve- " ments; for their avowed and proper ob- " ject is to reward or relieve indigent merit." But how fhall he find favour in the eyes of thofe who affume all publick virtue to themfelves and their party; and who are inca-

* Miles's Letter.

pable

pable of combining the efforts of a long life,
when its laſt act ſhall claſh with their views?
What merit ſhall he claim who ſeeks to root
up thoſe principles, and oppoſe thoſe prac-
tices, which would deprive the Crown of
the power and the means of rewarding or of
relieving indigent merit? Shall he then who
has laboured for the Publick go unrewarded,
becauſe it is dogmatically laid his remuneration, which he receives as the effect of
national gratitude, " cannot well be applied
to purpoſes of national improvement?"
Surely, the property thus honourably acquired is at leaſt as beneficial to the community as any perſonal property ariſing
from labour. It circulates as other monied
property: and if applied in the purchaſe
of lands, may, proportionably, become of
as great publick utility as the Bedford eſtates:
for, doubtleſs the " landed penſioner," would
take example from the noble Duke's prudence and patriotiſm, and render his property as productive as poſſible. But ſince
penſions are ſo obnoxious, in what way
would

would thefe faftidious gentlemen " reward or
relieve. indigent merit," or publick fervices?
Is the prefent mode more exceptionable than
confifcation and plunder? Or is it impoffible
to become publickly beneficial without adopting the cannibal philofophy of France; and
impoffible to reward fuch merit, but by a
diftribution of all property among all men*,
accord-

* This is ferioufly recommended in a " Warm Reply
to Mr. Burke, by A. Macleod :—" " All we have to do,"
fays this warm writer, " confifts in candidly acknowledg-
" ing the right of perfonal fecurity and perfonal comfort.
" If at prefent thefe are not enjoyed, prudence fhould dic-
" tate an immediate adoption of fuch regulations as would
" ultimately procure them. *Every fubject of thefe kingdoms,*
" *by a fair diftribution of the national purfe, might be raifed*
" *to honourable independence.* Now, however, a fervile
" coincidence with the nod of power alone diftinguifhes the
" fons of Britain. Mortifying condition ! abject men !"—
This gentleman writes a great deal about the " tree of
knowledge, original fin, and how " painful it is to be virtuous in this age."—He exclaims, " Ah! this age! Curfe
" the age, and curfe the people too, who can bafely com-
" promife their liberties for gold, and barter heaven for a
" curricle !"—He allows that he is fometimes *in a paffion :*
" If I were in a paffion, the criticks muft know, or if they
" will

according to the ftrict laws of Equality, and
the admirable inftitutes of the fans-culotte
code ?

The adverfaries of Mr. Burke are willing to
believe that his Penfion is given him for his
writings in favour of monarchy, and of the
war with France. But they are unable to
point out a paffage in thofe writings wherein
he

" will not, they, and the whole world may, that the ap-
" proaching diffolution of order, the approaching depreda-
" tion of humanity, the approaching funeral of Britain made
" me fo : and far from correcting thefe inbred tranfports,
" I yield to their fervour, I cherifh all their warmth ; they
" fhall animate my laft breath, and the gafp will be for li-
" berty!"—Could *Bully Bottom* † have faid more ?—But Mr.
Macleod is in a ftill greater paffion about liberty :—" Only
" fuch men as Mr. Burke," he fays, " would dare to af-
" fert, that Englifhmen owe their liberties to the Houfe of
" Orange. I declare that, when reading that affertion, I
" could not refift emotions at once indignant and fcornful :
" I even faid in my heart, *damn the man!*"—All this,
however, is to be forgiven, when we find the Author,
in a lucid interval, obferving, very truly, that his " con-
" clufions will be pronounced the ravings of a heated ima-
" gination, the dreams of an eager theorift, or the augur-
" ings of a difaffected man."—Doubtlefs, thefe caufes have,
jointly or feverally, produced the " *Warm Reply.*"

† Shakefpeare's Midfummer Night's Dream.

he has either injured or mifreprefented the
Conftitution of England. What he has faid in
regard to the monarchy of France, he will hardly
be induced to give up, till the profperity of
that country, under any other form of government, fhall compel him to renounce thofe
ideas which have been ftrengthened and con-
firmed by the uncontroulable events of feveral
fucceffive years. To the neceffity and the
juftice of our war with France neither the
friends nor the enemies of Mr. Burke are
ftrangers. That neceffity and that juftice have
been repeatedly demonftrated both in and out
of Parliament. They were, and yet are, inti-
mately felt by every man who has the leaft
fenfe of national honour, of general profperity,
or of focial rights. The meaneft peafant in
the kingdom, not infeċted with French madnefs, or the Old Jewry difeafe, felt an inftinc-
tive enmity againft the common foes of all civilized fociety. He felt that reafon and the
rights of human nature were violated and in-
vaded by a fierce banditti. All his moral
feelings were roufed. Even he comprehended,
becaufe he felt, that we warred not with principles,

ciples, merely fpcculative : that were indeed to
fight with phantoms ; but that we warred
with principles carried into practice : with
principles and opinions which urged a lawlefs
horde to rife againft the privileges and the
well-being of every community, and of all
mankind; and which it therefore became a
duty, and an indifpenfible neceffity, to oppofe.
He was ftimulated by the united energies of
the beft paffions to contend for the preferva-
tion of the beft and deareft rights : individual
felicity and focial happinefs. It was not with
him a conteft for power, for dominion, for
pre-eminence in the fcale of nations ; it was a
conteft to preferve the liberties, the religion,
the laws, the very exiftence of his own country, againft the invafion of an enthufiaftick,
and prefumptuous tyranny. The French Tree
of Liberty he wifhed not to fee planted in his
native foil. But, in proportion as he venerat-
ed the old Englifh Oak, he abhorred that noi-
fome exotick : the baleful Tree, with its poi-
fonous berries, and its deadly leaves ; for
he found wherever it ftruck its root, the paffing winds wafted from its noxious branches

L   peftilence

peftilence and death. He perceived himfelf
called upon not móre as a member of a great
kingdom, than as a man, to unite in refifting
thofe who had not only overthrown their own
government, and defolated their own country,
but invited, nay infifted on, furrounding nations, to join them in a general havock for
the deftruction of every thing facred and valu-
able to the human race. If what he felt was
ftrongly impreffed on the minds and hearts of
the people at large ; and that, with the exception of a few feditious clubs, cannot be con-
tradicted : if the Publick thus felt, without
adverting to the extenfive and important motives operating on the minds of Statefmen ;
Mr. Burke might reafonably conclude that the
heart of Lord Keppel, had he been living,
would have beat in unifon ; becaufe he was as
well politically as morally juft *. His honefty

was

---

* His Lordfhip was of a different opinion from one of
Mr. Burke's opponents: " I remember once dining with a
" gentleman who was formerly in Parliament, and with
" whom I have lived in habits of familiar intercourfe ;
" but he much fhocked me by queftioning the honefty of
" all

was indivifiblc. He had not one fyftem of ethicks for his publick, and another for his his private, conduct. A nobleman poffefling fuch a mind, influenced by fuch principles, would fcarcely have been devoid of thofe fen-'fations which evidently pervaded the breaft of every man in Europe, who had the leaft pre-
tenfion

" all men in politicks: *arguing from my own feelings, and re-*
" *ferring him to my own hiftory* †, I fupported a contrary
" opinion. Experience, however, has convinced me, that
" my friend, although far from being right to the full ex-
" tent of his affertion, knew mankind much better than
" I did."
Miles's Letter.

† I will not fay any thing of Mr. Miles's *egotifm*, of which this is but as a grain from a mountain : neither will I afk whether he now refers to his own experience, his own feelings, or his own hiftory, for a confirmation of his friend's knowledge of mankind: I will only fay, that there cannot be a pofition more falfe, or more dangerous, than this of univerfal depravity. When fuch ideas are diffeminated by men who are fuppofed to know the world, as the ideas of higher claffes of fociety, thofe of the lower think themfelves authorized to hold the fame opinions, and to practife upon them. He who has a bad opinion of mankind cannot be furprized if mankind have no good opinion of him.

tenfion to a regard for juftice or humanity. In proportion as his Lordfhip's regard for ineftimable qualities was ftronger than thofe of ordinary men, fo much more ftrongly would he have felt the neceffity and the juftice of the war: for he well knew, that not to go againft fleets of pirates, and armies of robbers, were to countenance them; and that he who is carelefs of the inftitutions of other governments and of neighbouring ftates, cannot be fuppofed friendly to any government; fince he evinces a willingnefs to fanction a conduct tending to the deftruction of all.

But we are told, that the French have given up their moft flagitious principles, and renounced the "glorious idea" of reducing all eftablifhed governments to the level of their own miferable chaos; and that, therefore, we fhould attend to terms of peace. It is well for THEM, if they have done fo. But how far that confideration ought to induce this country to abandon the war, without accomplifhing its original object: how far the fecondary confideration of expence, ought to induce us to facrifice the dignity and the glory

of

of the country, by accepting of difgraceful terms, or of any terms, fhort of the moft advantageous and the moft honourable ; muft be left for thofe fubfequent difcullions in which the obfervations of Mr. Adair * and others may find fome attention.

Meanwhile, let it always be recollected that, whoever fhall be refponfible, the war was unavoidable. " Formerly," fays Mr. Burke, in addreffing himfelf to a Gentleman in Paris, " formerly your affairs were your own concern only. We felt for them as men ; but we kept aloof from them, becaufe we were not citizens of France. But when we fee the model held up to ourfelves, we muft feel as Englifhmen, and feeling, we muft provide as Englifhmen. *Your affairs, in fpite of us, are made a part of our intereft ;* fo far at leaft as to keep at a diftance your panacea, or your plague. If it be a panacea, we do not want it : we know the confequences of unneceffary phyfick. If it be a plague, it is fuch a plague,

---

* See Part of a Letter from Robert Adair, Efq. to the Right Hon. Charles James Fox.

that

that the precautions of the moſt ſevere quaran-
tine ought to be eſtabliſhed againſt it." *   Several of Mr. Burke's opponents contend that
the war was neceſſary : neither party prejudice
nor falſe philoſophy having ſuperſeded, in this
inſtance, their natural ſenſe of right and wrong.

When it is conſidéred who and what they
are that have brought the preſent calamities
upon their own country, upon this country,
and upon Europe in general : that, in imita-
tion of the moſt diſgraceful act recorded in
Engliſh hiſtory, they have murdered their
King ; thereby giving a horrid teſtimony of
their renunciation of every thing ſacred and
binding among men : that they murdered a
Queen, whoſe only fault was that, if ſhe had
the influence ſhe is believed to have had, ſhe
did not exert it to yoke the wolves howling to
devour her : that they murdered a Princeſs and
a Prince, equally innocent, the Siſter and the
Son of theſe illuſtrious ſufferers : that, not
content with thus ſhedding the Royal blood of
their own country, they incited, and offered
to aid and aſſiſt other countries, particularly

* Reflections.

this

this kingdom, to commit the like enormities, and to lay wafte the whole religious and moral, civil and political world : when thefe things are at all confidered, with the circumftances attached to them, it cannot be thought furprifing that Mr. Burke fhould exprefs his abhorrence of a Peace with Regicide. He has been cenfured as the author of a war that was unavoidable. It is a cenfure which, however juft or erroneous, does him honour. He is thus cenfured for being a friend to the human race, and efpecially to Great Britain, the total overthrow of whofe Government was not lefs the object of Conventional determination, both at home and abroad, than the extinction of the French monarchy.—If his labours have contributed to create him perfonal enemies among thofe who wifh to reduce their new principles to practice, Mr. Burke muft reft fatisfied with the approbation of all fuch as feel a real concern for the fafety and happinefs of the country.

THE END.

This Day is Published, Price 1s.

THE SECOND EDITION OF

Mr. BURKE's

CONDUCT and PRETENSIONS

CONSIDERED:

WITH

ILLUSTRATIVE ANECDOTES.

BY A *ROYALIST.*

* 9 7 8 3 3 3 7 1 9 5 6 1 8 *